4

FRONTIER
Thunder at Dawn